EVANSTON PUBLIC LIBRARY
W9-BHL-819

OCT 3 1 1995

SUMMER LEGS

SUMMER LEGS

by Anita Hakkinen
illustrated by Abby Carter

Henry Holt and Company • New York

Henry Holt and Company, Inc.
Publishers since 1866
115 West 18th Street
New York, New York 10011

Henry Holt is a registered
trademark of Henry Holt and Company, Inc.

Published in Canada by Fitzhenry & Whiteside Ltd.,
195 Allstate Parkway, Markham, Ontario L3R 4T8.

Library of Congress Cataloging-in-Publication Data
Hakkinen, Anita. Summer legs / by Anita Hakkinen; illustrated by Abby Carter.
Summary: Verses describe "summer legs" engaging in activities
such as swimming, tree climbing, playing, and picnicking.
[1. Leg—Fiction. 2. Stories in rhyme.] I. Carter, Abby, ill.
II. Title. PZ8.3.H124Su 1994 [E]—dc20 94-25838
ISBN 0-8050-2262-7
First Edition—1995
Printed in the United States of America
on acid-free paper. ∞

1 3 5 7 9 10 8 6 4 2

The artist used watercolors and gouache
on Arches cold-press watercolor paper to
create the illustrations for this book.

For Dave, Dan, Dale, Alana, and
Darren, my brothers and sister,
and for my children, Ryan and Andi

—A. H.

For Doug, Samantha, and Willie

—A. C.

Nice to see you summer legs
Sunshine splashy summer legs
Busy breezy over easy
Splendid summer legs.

Dangling are my summer legs
Drifting lifting summer legs
Flailing sailing first-class mailing
Jungle-gymmie legs.

Drippy are my summer legs
Tricky kicky summer legs
Flipping flops and daring drops
Swimming-pooly legs.

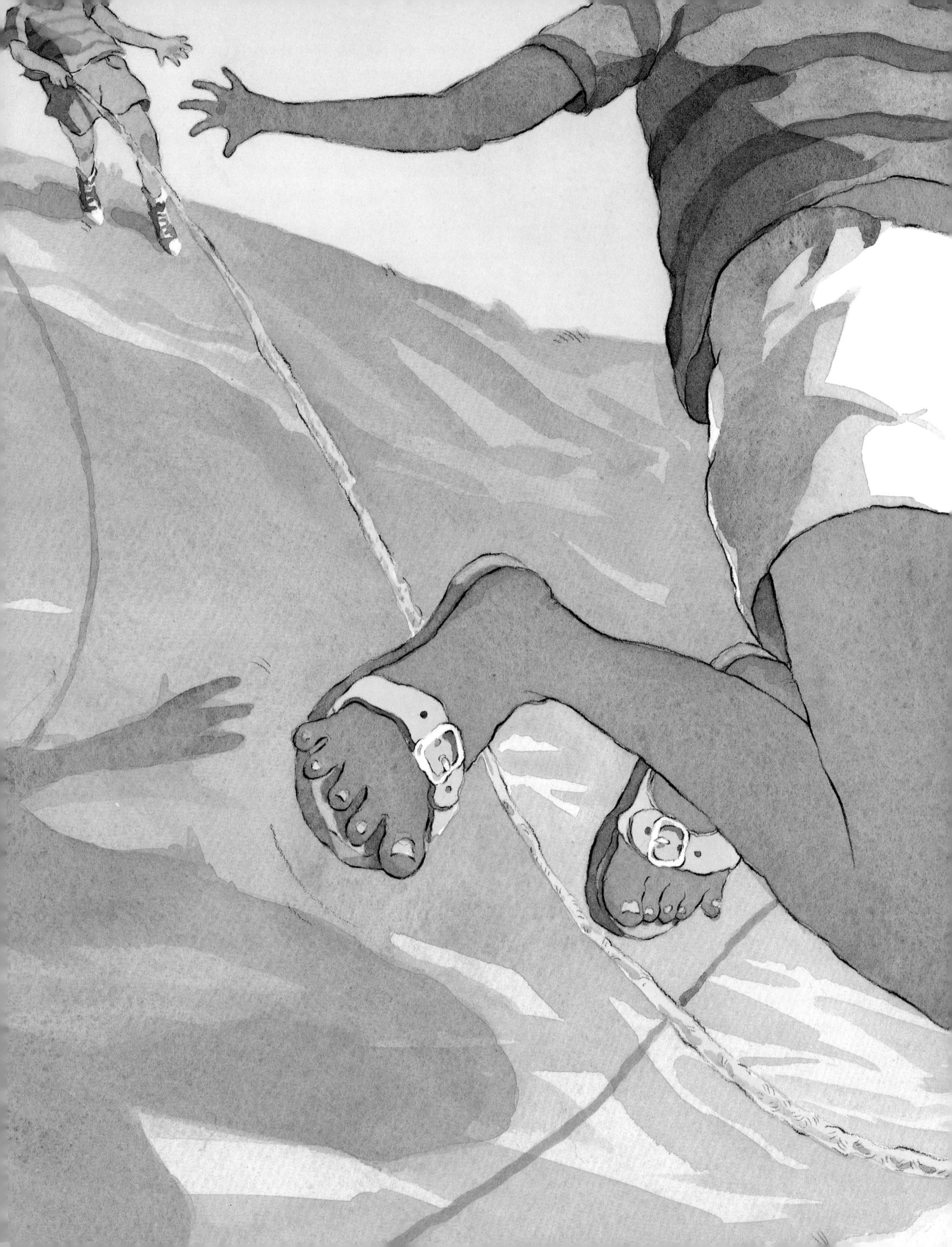

Bouncy are my summer legs
Sassy skipping summer legs
Reflex rhyming perfect timing
High jump-roping legs.

FLIES

Itchy are my summer legs
Scratchy patchy summer legs
Mini mites with tiny bites
'Skeeto-got-me legs.

Flying are my summer legs
To the sky my summer legs
Kicking crowds of curly clouds
Backyard swinging legs.

Spicy are my summer legs
Tingy tangy summer legs
Sloppy sticky mustard drippy
Family picnic legs.

Sandy are my summer legs
Seashell-sprinkled summer legs
Beachy bummy ho-humdrummy
At-the-ocean legs.

Straddling are my summer legs
Bolting bark now summer legs
Scraping bruising chancy cruising
Tall tree-climbing legs.

GHOST STORIES

Toasty are my summer legs
Hot dog roasty summer legs
Kindling crackling snapping clapping
Golden campfire legs.

Speckled are my summer legs
Funny-freckled summer legs
Dribble drap and spiddle splat
Front-porch-painting legs.

Soily are my summer legs
Leafy labor summer legs
Tickly hugs from blooms and bugs
Garden-weeding legs.

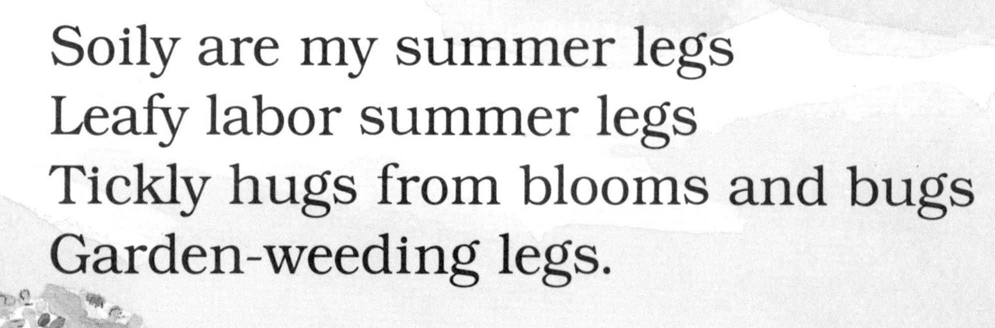

Sprinting are my summer legs
Reeling stealing summer legs
Anxious inning sliding winning
Baseball-playing legs.

Nice to know you summer legs
Run for shelter summer legs
Change your ways for chilly days
Good-bye summer legs!